Aubie's
Journey Through
The Yellowhammer State

Aimee Aryal

Illustrated by Gabhor Utomo

www.mascotbooks.com

Auburn, Alabama is the proud home of Auburn University.

Aubie was enjoying a relaxing summer on the campus of Auburn University. With football season fast approaching, Aubie decided to take one last summer vacation. He thought it would be great fun to journey throughout the Yellowhammer State, where he could see many interesting places and make new friends along the way.

Before leaving campus, Aubie strolled past Samford Hall. Auburn fans waved to him and yelled, "Hello, Aubie! War Eagle!"

On his way out of town, Aubie passed through Toomer's Corner, where he saw more friends. His friends wished him well and said, "Enjoy your trip, Aubie!"

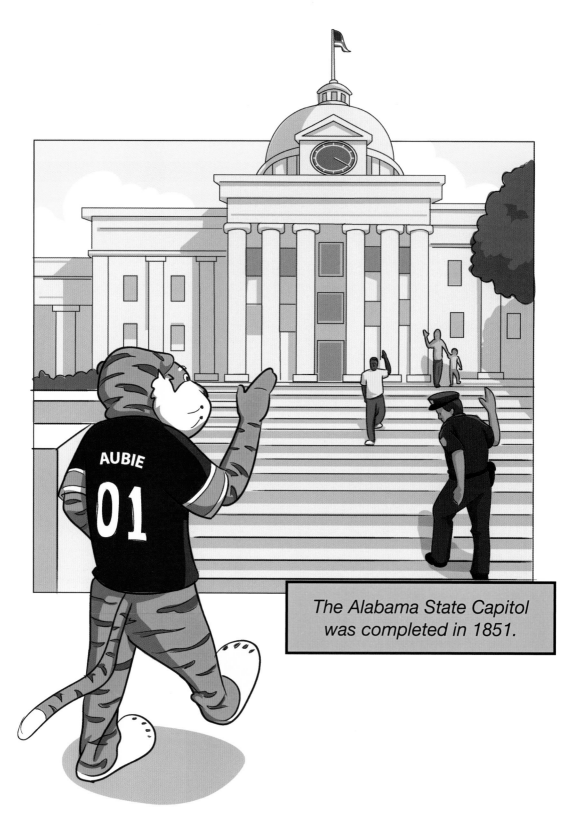

The Alabama State Capitol was completed in 1851.

From campus, Aubie made the short trip to Montgomery, the capital of the Yellowhammer State. He was impressed at the size of the Alabama State Capitol. He saw a police officer on the steps who waved and called, "Hello, Aubie! War Eagle!"

He then went to the Montgomery Zoo, where he saw many different animals, including zebras. "Look, Aubie, they look like referees!" said one of his young friends.

Next, Aubie was off to Shakespeare Gardens, where he performed with the other actors. After a splendid performance, the crowd cheered, "Bravo, Aubie!"

Old Alabama Town is a collection of restored 19th-century buildings in Montgomery, Alabama.

Aubie traveled to Old Alabama Town, where life was still like it was in the 19th century. Aubie put on the clothes of the time and strolled through the village. Aubie was amazed by how much daily life had changed!

Aubie stopped by one of the factories in Old Alabama Town, where he saw an old cotton gin weaving the crops into clothing. Aubie asked the worker if he could make him a blue and orange shirt. The worker smiled and said, "Go, Tigers!"

The racetrack at Talladega is over 2 ½ miles long, with capacity for over 175,000 race fans.

Aubie was enjoying his leisurely drive through the Yellowhammer State. However, he was ready to pick up the pace. At the world famous Talladega Superspeedway, Aubie took a victory lap around the track! As he passed by the crowded stands, race fans yelled, "War Eagle!"

When the race began, Aubie joined a pit crew and provided a helping hand. Afterward, Aubie joined a friendly tailgate party, where he enjoyed good food and great company. Some of Aubie's new friends took him to the nearby International Motorsports Hall of Fame & Museum, where he learned about the sport's great history.

At the Anniston Museum of Natural History, Aubie learned so many interesting facts about the world. He came across a family of Auburn fans. They sure were happy to see Aubie! As they walked by, they said, "Hello, Aubie!"

Inside the museum, Aubie joined an archaeologist and the two checked out the mummy exhibit. "Those mummies sure are old," Aubie thought. Next, he went off to see the African savannah exhibit, and got a glimpse of his least favorite animal – an elephant!

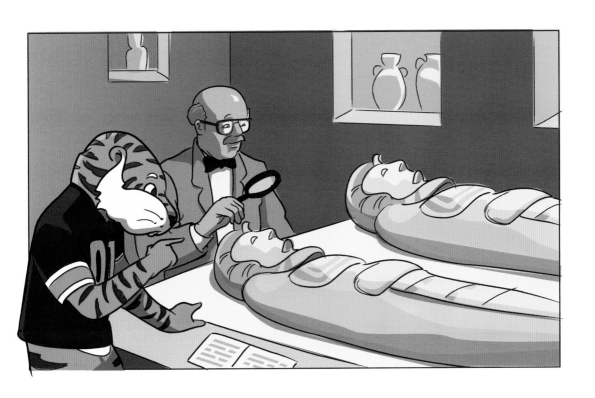

Aubie enjoyed spending time in the great outdoors, so he headed off to Lake Guntersville State Park. He went bass fishing and caught a big one! The fish said in a worried voice, "Hello, Aubie!"

Aubie also went sailing. It was so peaceful on the lake. Finally, he rode his jet ski and saw some Tiger fans. The fans waved to Aubie and shouted out, "War Eagle!"

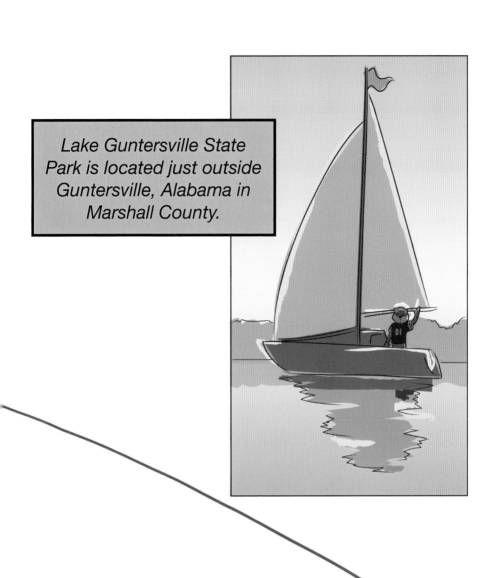

Lake Guntersville State Park is located just outside Guntersville, Alabama in Marshall County.

Aubie continued north to Huntsville. Aubie strolled through Big Spring Park and enjoyed fabulous views of the city. Standing on the Japanese Bridge, Aubie spotted ducks, fish, and of course, more Auburn fans. The people nearby were thrilled to see him and called out, "Hello, Aubie!"

Aubie's next stop was Rocket Park. He met a very smart scientist there who gave him a tour and told the mascot all about rockets and space travel. When Aubie thanked him for being a great tour guide, the scientist smiled and said, "War Eagle, Aubie!"

From 1948 to 1988 Legion Field hosted the annual Alabama vs. Auburn football game nicknamed the "Iron Bowl."

Aubie drove south to Birmingham, where he stopped at historic Legion Field, the site of so many exciting Auburn football games. Outside the stadium, fans noticed the mascot and called, "Hello, Aubie!"

Next, Aubie got all dressed up in a tuxedo and conducted the Alabama Symphony Orchestra. The crowd cheered, "Bravo, Aubie!"

Ready to pick up the beat, Aubie broke out his electric guitar and performed at City Stages, Birmingham's famous music festival. "Rock on, Aubie!" roared his fans.

Finally, he stopped at Vulcan Park and admired the statue with a young friend who said, "Hello, Aubie!"

Standing 56 feet tall and weighing over 100,000 pounds, Birmingham's Vulcan Statue is the largest cast iron statue in the world.

Aubie just couldn't resist driving over to Tuscaloosa!
Being on the campus of the University of Alabama
made Aubie feel a little uneasy. Although he tried,
it was difficult for the tiger mascot to go unnoticed
in 'Bama territory. Fortunately, as he walked by
Denny Chimes, he saw a fellow Auburn fan. The fan
smiled and whispered, "Hello, Aubie."

Tuscaloosa is the home of the University of Alabama.

Mobile is on the Gulf of Mexico and is Alabama's only seaport.

Aubie continued south all the way to Mobile, where he visited the USS Alabama Museum in Mobile Bay. From there, it was a short trip to Bellingrath Gardens and Home, where he admired the beautiful flowers. A bee buzzed, "Hello, Aubie!"

Thrilled about being on the Gulf of Mexico, Aubie went to Dauphin Island, where he lounged on the beach, built himself a sandcastle, and played in the water with some Auburn fans. The fans cheered, "War Eagle!"

Aubie was ready for a round of golf! He traveled to Dothan and played one of the courses on the famous Robert Trent Jones Golf Trail. Aubie took a swing, but the only thing that went flying was his golf club! "Fore!" yelled his caddy.

After the round of golf, Aubie stopped at a nearby pool to have fun and go swimming with his new friends. As he splashed into the pool, his pals yelled, "Cannonball, Aubie!"

Having traveled all over the entire state, Aubie finally made it back to Auburn University. What a great vacation it had been! All his fans were thrilled at his return and cheered, "Hello, Aubie! Welcome home!"

At last, back in his own room, Aubie thought about all the interesting places he visited and the great friends he made along the way. He crawled into his own bed and fell fast asleep.

Good night, Aubie!

Aubie's
Journey Through
The Yellowhammer State

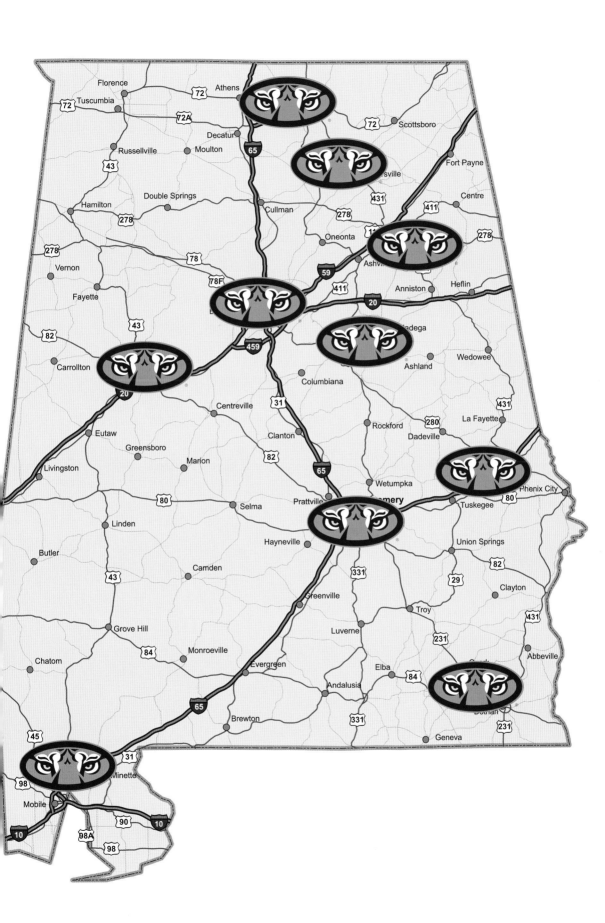

For Anna and Maya. ~ Aimee Aryal

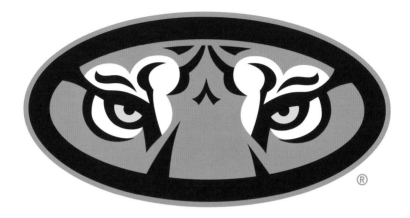

For more information about our products,
please visit us online at www.mascotbooks.com.

For more information, please contact Mascot Books,
P.O. Box 220157, Chantilly, VA 20153-0157

ISBN: 978-1-934878-33-0

Printed in the United States.

www.mascotbooks.com

Title List

Major League Baseball

Boston Red Sox	Hello, *Wally*!	Jerry Remy
Boston Red Sox	*Wally The Green Monster* And His Journey Through *Red Sox Nation*!	Jerry Remy
Boston Red Sox	Coast to Coast with *Wally The Green Monster*	Jerry Remy
Boston Red Sox	A Season with *Wally The Green Monster*	Jerry Remy
Colorado Rockies	Hello, *Dinger*!	Aimee Aryal
Detroit Tigers	Hello, *Paws*!	Aimee Aryal
New York Yankees	Let's Go, *Yankees*!	Yogi Berra
New York Yankees	*Yankees Town*	Aimee Aryal
New York Mets	Hello, *Mr. Met*!	Rusty Staub
New York Mets	*Mr. Met* and his Journey Through the Big Apple	Aimee Aryal
St. Louis Cardinals	Hello, *Fredbird*!	Ozzie Smith
Philadelphia Phillies	Hello, *Phillie Phanatic*!	Aimee Aryal
Chicago Cubs	Let's Go, *Cubs*!	Aimee Aryal
Chicago White Sox	Let's Go, *White Sox*!	Aimee Aryal
Cleveland Indians	Hello, *Slider*!	Bob Feller
Seattle Mariners	Hello, *Mariner Moose*!	Aimee Aryal
Washington Nationals	Hello, *Screech*!	Aimee Aryal
Milwaukee Brewers	Hello, *Bernie Brewer*!	Aimee Aryal

College

Alabama	Hello, Big Al!	Aimee Aryal
Alabama	Roll Tide!	Ken Stabler
Alabama	Big Al's Journey Through the Yellowhammer State	Aimee Aryal
Arizona	Hello, Wilbur!	Lute Olson
Arkansas	Hello, Big Red!	Aimee Aryal
Arkansas	Big Red's Journey Through the Razorback State	Aimee Aryal
Auburn	Hello, Aubie!	Aimee Aryal
Auburn	War Eagle!	Pat Dye
Auburn	Aubie's Journey Through the Yellowhammer State	Aimee Aryal
Boston College	Hello, Baldwin!	Aimee Aryal
Brigham Young	Hello, Cosmo!	LaVell Edwards
Cal - Berkeley	Hello, Oski!	Aimee Aryal
Clemson	Hello, Tiger!	Aimee Aryal
Clemson	Tiger's Journey Through the Palmetto State	Aimee Aryal
Colorado	Hello, Ralphie!	Aimee Aryal
Connecticut	Hello, Jonathan!	Aimee Aryal
Duke	Hello, Blue Devil!	Aimee Aryal
Florida	Hello, Albert!	Aimee Aryal
Florida State	Let's Go, 'Noles!	Aimee Aryal
Georgia	Hello, Hairy Dawg!	Aimee Aryal
Georgia	How 'Bout Them Dawgs!	Aimee Aryal
Georgia	Hairy Dawg's Journey Through the Peach State	Vince Dooley
Georgia Tech	Hello, Buzz!	
Gonzaga	Spike, The Gonzaga Bulldog	Aimee Aryal / Mike Pringle
Illinois	Let's Go, Illini!	
Indiana	Let's Go, Hoosiers!	Aimee Aryal
Iowa	Hello, Herky!	Aimee Aryal
Iowa State	Hello, Cy!	Aimee Aryal
James Madison	Hello, Duke Dog!	Amy DeLashmutt
Kansas	Hello, Big Jay!	Aimee Aryal
Kansas State	Hello, Willie!	Aimee Aryal
Kentucky	Hello, Wildcat!	Dan Walter
LSU	Hello, Mike!	Aimee Aryal
LSU	Mike's Journey Through the Bayou State	Aimee Aryal
Maryland	Hello, Testudo!	
Michigan	Let's Go, Blue!	Aimee Aryal
Michigan State	Hello, Sparty!	Aimee Aryal
Minnesota	Hello, Goldy!	Aimee Aryal
Mississippi	Hello, Colonel Rebel!	Aimee Aryal
Mississippi State	Hello, Bully!	Aimee Aryal

Pro Football

Carolina Panthers	Let's Go, Panthers!	Aimee Aryal
Chicago Bears	Let's Go, Bears!	Aimee Aryal
Dallas Cowboys	How 'Bout Them Cowboys!	Aimee Aryal
Green Bay Packers	Go, Pack, Go!	Aimee Aryal
Kansas City Chiefs	Let's Go, Chiefs!	Aimee Aryal
Minnesota Vikings	Let's Go, Vikings!	Aimee Aryal
New York Giants	Let's Go, Giants!	Aimee Aryal
New York Jets	J-E-T-S! Jets, Jets, Jets!	Aimee Aryal
New England Patriots	Let's Go, Patriots!	Aimee Aryal
Pittsburgh Steelers	Here We Go Steelers!	Aimee Aryal
Seattle Seahawks	Let's Go, Seahawks!	Aimee Aryal
Washington Redskins	Hail To The Redskins!	Aimee Aryal

Basketball

Dallas Mavericks	Let's Go, Mavs!	Mark Cuban
Boston Celtics	Let's Go, Celtics!	Aimee Aryal

Other

Kentucky Derby	White Diamond Runs For The Roses	Aimee Aryal
Marine Corps Marathon	Run, Miles, Run!	Aimee Aryal

Missouri	Hello, Truman!	Aimee Aryal
Nebraska	Hello, Herbie Husker!	Todd Donoho
North Carolina	Hello, Rameses!	Aimee Aryal
North Carolina	Rameses' Journey Through the Tar Heel State	Aimee Aryal
North Carolina St.	Hello, Mr. Wuf!	
North Carolina St.	Mr. Wuf's Journey Through North Carolina	Aimee Aryal
Notre Dame	Let's Go, Irish!	
Ohio State	Hello, Brutus!	Aimee Aryal
Ohio State	Brutus' Journey	Aimee Aryal
Oklahoma	Let's Go, Sooners!	Aimee Aryal
Oklahoma State	Hello, Pistol Pete!	Aimee Aryal
Oregon	Go Ducks!	Aimee Aryal
Oregon State	Hello, Benny the Beaver!	Aimee Aryal
Penn State	Hello, Nittany Lion!	Aimee Aryal
Penn State	We Are Penn State!	Aimee Aryal
Purdue	Hello, Purdue Pete!	Joe Paterno
Rutgers	Hello, Scarlet Knight!	Aimee Aryal
South Carolina	Hello, Cocky!	Aimee Aryal
South Carolina	Cocky's Journey Through the Palmetto State	Aimee Aryal
So. California	Hello, Tommy Trojan!	
Syracuse	Hello, Otto!	Aimee Aryal
Tennessee	Hello, Smokey!	Aimee Aryal
Tennessee	Smokey's Journey Through the Volunteer State	Aimee Aryal
Texas	Hello, Hook 'Em!	
Texas	Hook 'Em's Journey Through the Lone Star State	Aimee Aryal
Texas A & M	Howdy, Reveille!	
Texas A & M	Reveille's Journey Through the Lone Star State	Aimee Aryal
Texas Tech	Hello, Masked Rider!	
UCLA	Hello, Joe Bruin!	Aimee Aryal
Virginia	Hello, CavMan!	Aimee Aryal
Virginia Tech	Hello, Hokie Bird!	Aimee Aryal
Virginia Tech	Yea, It's Hokie Game Day!	Aimee Aryal
Virginia Tech	Hokie Bird's Journey Through Virginia	Frank Beamer / Aimee Aryal
Wake Forest	Hello, Demon Deacon!	
Washington	Hello, Harry the Husky!	Aimee Aryal
Washington State	Hello, Butch!	Aimee Aryal
West Virginia	Hello, Mountaineer!	Aimee Aryal
Wisconsin	Hello, Bucky!	Aimee Aryal
Wisconsin	Bucky's Journey Through the Badger State	Aimee Aryal

Order online at **mascotbooks.com** using promo code " **free**" to receive **FREE SHIPPING!**

More great titles coming soon!

info@mascotbooks.com

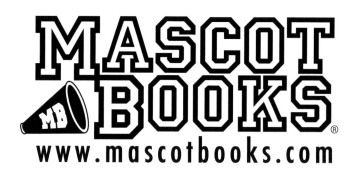
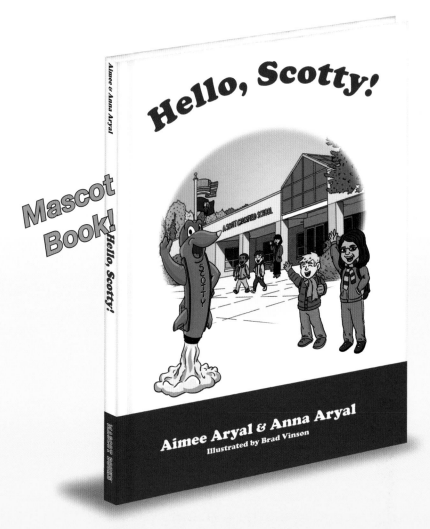

Let Mascot Books create a customized children's book for your school or team!

Here's how our fundraisers work ...

- **Mascot Books creates a customized children's book with content specific to your school. When parents buy your school's book,** your organization earns cash!

- **When parents buy any of Mascot Books' college or professional team books,** your organization earns more cash!

- **We also offer options for a customized plush, apparel, and even mascot costumes!**

Mascot Costumes!

Dougie the Dragon

Mascot T-Shirts!

Proud to be a Vincent Elementary Duck!

Vinny the Duck

Mascot Plush!

Lulu the Ladybug

For more information about the most innovative fundraiser on the market, contact us at info@mascotbooks.com.